Ghosting

keith gray

For the Fassls

First published in 2008 in Great Britain by
Barrington Stoke Ltd
18 Walker Street, Edinburgh, EH3 7LP

www.barringtonstoke.co.uk

This edition first published 2012
Reprinted 2018

A CIP catalogue record for this book is available
from the British Library upon request

ISBN: 978-1-78112-081-1

Printed in Great Britain by Charlesworth Press

Contents

Chapter 1
The House on Turn Lane

Everyone said my mother had a gift. They said she could talk to the dead. And they said my sister, Sandy, had the gift too.

Mrs Mory wanted Sandy to talk to her dead husband for her. Mrs Mory was an old lady who lived in an older house at the far end of Turn Lane. Sandy and I went to the house on a cold Sunday afternoon in November.

"Come in, come in," Mrs Mory said as she opened the door. "This way, leave the cold out there. That's right. Everyone's here. We're all waiting."

Sandy put her hand on my arm. "This is my brother Nat," she said to Mrs Mory as we went in. "I hope it's OK if he comes too? I like him to be with me."

It was a bright day outside, but inside it was dim and dark. All of the curtains in the house had been closed. It took a second or two to see anything in the gloom.

Mrs Mory took us down a long narrow hall-way. Just by the front door was a small table with an old telephone on it. There were some droopy flowers in a jug, too, and a short, fancy lamp with a big shade. Along one wall there were rows and rows of bookshelves, all packed full with dusty books. On the very top shelf was a stuffed fox that stared down at us with glassy eyes. The wall on the other side of the hall-way had loads of photos hanging on it – all in frames. Some of the photos were colour, but most of them were black-and-white snapshots of people from a long time ago.

Sandy stopped to peer at them. "Is one of these a picture of your husband, Mrs Mory?" she asked.

"Yes, that's right. That's him there," Mrs Mory said, and she pointed at a black-and-white picture of a young man in uniform. "He was a pilot, you know. And here's a photo of him when we were on holiday in France." She pointed at a colour photo. "And here he is with our grand-children. That one was taken the year before he died. He was nearly 80 then, but I'll always remember him as the handsome pilot I first met all those years ago."

Sandy smiled. "What a handsome man," she said. She touched each photo in turn with her finger-tips. "And his pictures give off a wonderful energy. Don't you think so, Nat?" she asked me.

I nodded. I knew what she meant.

Mrs Mory smiled too. Then she went on down the hall-way. "This way, please."

She was a short woman with lots of grey hair. My sister was much taller than her. Sandy had a way of walking that made it look as if she was floating. The long, dark skirt she always wore brushed against the floor, and hid her feet. Her blonde hair fell all the way down her back. She was seventeen but people often thought she was older. I was fifteen and I looked fifteen. No one would think I was older – I was far too spotty and clumsy.

We went into a dark dining room at the end of the hall-way. There were three people already sitting at the table. A bald man with a big white face like a moon and little round wire glasses sat next to a girl who wasn't much older than Sandy. She looked tense and upset. On her finger was a chunky gold ring and she kept fiddling with it, twisting it round and round.

"This is Mr Coil," Mrs Mory said. "We go to the same church. And this is my niece, Miss Fay."

Moon-faced Mr Coil nodded and said hello. Behind his glasses he had tiny, dark, piggy eyes. He was sweating and kept patting a handkerchief over his damp, shiny face.

Miss Fay gave a nervous smile. "I'm Emma," she said softly. She only looked at Sandy and me for a split second before she started to play with the ring on her finger again.

The third person sat across the table from Miss Fay and Mr Coil. She was a big woman in a horrible hat. Mrs Mory turned to her. "This is my good friend and neighbour Mrs Tucker," she said.

When Mrs Tucker smiled she showed all her teeth. They were yellow and stained by cigarettes. Her hat looked as if there was a dead garden on her head. "I've been so very much looking forward to this afternoon," Mrs Tucker said. Her voice was the poshest I think I'd ever heard. "Oh, yes," she went on, "hardly slept a wink last night. I've been so very, very excited."

Sandy thanked everyone for coming and sat down at the top of the table. She pulled her long skirt in around her chair. Mrs Mory sat next to Mrs Tucker on one side, with Mr Coil and Emma Fay on the other. I stayed standing behind Sandy.

"We should begin as soon as we can," Sandy said. "I can already feel the dead pushing to get in. Can you feel it too?"

There was a candle-holder with three candles in the middle of the dining table. Mrs Mory took out some matches to light them.

"I'd rather we used a light bulb," Sandy said. "Just a normal light bulb, if that's OK."

Mrs Mory was a little shocked. "A light bulb? Are you sure?"

"I often find they work best," Sandy said.

Mrs Mory still wasn't sure. She frowned and looked at Mrs Tucker. "I'm sure the young lady knows best," Mrs Tucker said. "She's done this a lot more than any of us."

Mrs Mory looked up at the light hanging from the ceiling. With a sigh she started to get up onto her chair to try and reach it.

"What about the bulb in the lamp by the front door?" I said. "In the hall-way? I can get it." I stepped quickly out of the dining room to fetch it.

While I was in the hall-way I heard them asking Sandy lots of questions. She answered as many of them as she could. But she wanted to explain things in her own way.

"I know there are a lot of different names for what we hope will happen this afternoon," she said. "But my mother always called it Ghosting. And my brother and I learned everything we know from my mother, so we call it Ghosting too."

"That's as good a name as any," Mr Coil said. He said it in a jokey way. But no one laughed.

"I can't promise that anything will happen," Sandy said, "but I'll try my best. And I'd better warn you that I can't control the dead. If they do use me to talk to you, I can't promise you'll like what they have to say."

I came back into the room then and put the bulb on the table in front of Sandy. I saw there was a gap in the curtains which let a line of sunlight sneak in. I pulled the curtains shut to block any hint of the world outside and keep the room as dark as possible.

I looked at the people sitting around the table. Mrs Mory and Mrs Tucker were excited, like kids on Christmas Eve. Mr Coil was sweating hard. His big moon-face looked like butter. Emma Fay was still very nervous. She gripped the edge of the table.

"You'll be fine, Emma," Mr Coil whispered, leaning in close to her. "Everything will be fine." He put his big hand on top of hers. But she jerked her hand away.

"Let us begin," Sandy said. "The energy in this house feels very strong. I can tell it has seen many lives. And many deaths."

Chapter 2
Ghosting

When Mum talked to the dead, she always did all of the "Is there anyone out there?" stuff. Some days she even went in for a whole load of weeping and wailing and swaying about. It was what people expected.

Sandy doesn't do any of that. She stays very still, very calm. I think she's much spookier.

Sandy asked the four people all sitting around the table to hold hands. Mrs Mory, Mrs Tucker and Mr Coil all did so quickly. Emma Fay didn't want to at first. She bit her bottom lip, took a deep breath, fiddled with her gold ring. I wasn't sure if she was worried about the Ghosting, or just didn't want to hold Mr Coil's sweaty hand.

"One thing I can promise," Sandy said to her, "is that I won't let anything harm you. Keep the circle of hands and you'll be safe."

Emma Fay nodded slowly. She flicked her hair out of her eyes and with another deep breath she put her hand across the table to hold Mrs Tucker's hand.

"Be brave," Mr Coil whispered. He took hold of her other hand.

I watched from the corner of the room. Sandy picked up the light bulb from the table, and tilted her head back. The four people around the table didn't dare take their eyes off her. The room was very dark but I could still see their faces. All of them looked excited – nervous and hopeful at the same time.

"Please think of the ones you love," Sandy said. "Think of the people you miss, the people you'd like me to contact for you."

She closed her eyes tight. "I can feel so much energy," she said. "It's like a mist. I can feel it swirling around me. This house has seen laughter and tears, hope and pain. And death. It's all trapped inside these walls. It's ... It's a thick mist of memory. I can feel ... I can feel ..."

And suddenly, in the dimness of the room, the light bulb Sandy was holding began to glow. Even though it wasn't plugged in and there were no wires or electricity, the bulb got brighter and brighter.

Everyone gasped. Emma Fay jumped up out of her chair.

"Please stay sitting," I said. "You shouldn't disturb my sister while she's Ghosting. It could be dangerous."

Emma Fay sat back down slowly. Mr Coil tugged at her hand. She reached out for Mrs Tucker's hand again. The moment she did, the noises started.

There was a tap, or a knock. A clunk – as if something was trapped inside the wood of the table and was trying to get out. The four people sitting around the table were quick to move back. Their chairs scraped on the floor as they moved as far back from the table as they could. But they kept hold of each other's hands. They were all staring at the table as the knocking came again. This time it was sharper, louder. Now it wasn't only Emma Fay who was scared. The dead were coming, and everyone could hear them with their own ears.

Sandy sat perfectly still, head back, eyes closed. She held the bright bulb in her finger-tips. It made long shadows on the walls of the room. She was moving her mouth, but no words were coming out. Not yet.

The clunking and knocking was getting louder. The four people around the table didn't know where to look. At the table? What if something really did burst out of the wood? Or at my sister? What if she started to talk?

The noises got worse. An awful sound filled the room. It was like screeching and scratching on metal. Like metal being scraped against metal. It was like a cry from another world, and it pushed icy needles into your ears and pricked all along your spine.

Mrs Mory put her hands to her ears.

"No!" I shouted. "No! Please keep holding hands. You mustn't break the circle!"

Mrs Tucker grabbed Mrs Mory's hand so hard it made Mrs Mory yelp.

And the split second she did, the noises stopped.

The room was silent again. No one dared say a word.

The four people looked dazed. Emma Fay was shaking. Mrs Tucker's hat was crooked. It had slipped to one side on her head. Mr Coil licked his lips twice, three times, looking around the room. No one knew what to do.

At last Mrs Mory asked, "Have I ...? Was it my fault ...?"

But my sister was looking at them now. Her eyes were wide and unblinking. The room was dark except for the light bulb Sandy held. She said, "There is someone else in the room with us. Someone who is no longer living."

The metal scraping noise started again and then hushed.

The four people around the table all held their breath. I'd been Ghosting with my mum and sister often enough to know that they would be gripping each other's hands so hard it would hurt. But I also knew that they'd never dream of letting go – not now.

"Is ... is it my husband?" Mrs Mory asked.

Sandy ignored her. Instead she looked at Emma Fay. "They have come for you."

The young woman gave a shudder. Her face was pale in the light from the bulb my sister held. "Who ... who is it?" Her voice was a tight whisper.

"They say they miss you very much," Sandy told her. "They are sorry you are still so sad."

Emma Fay leaned forward in her chair. "Is it Billy?" she whispered.

Sandy nodded. "Billy wants you to know he's all right. He misses you, but he's all right."

"Tell him ... Tell him I love him," Emma Fay said.

Sandy nodded again. "He knows. He says he gave you something. A gift?"

Emma Fay had tears in her eyes. "My ring. He gave me my ring."

"He says you should keep it forever, and he will forever be with you," Sandy told her.

Then Sandy slowly turned her head to stare at Mrs Mory. "Billy says hello to you too, Mrs Mory. He says he knows where your husband is. But Billy says Mr Mory cannot be here with us."

"But I want to speak to my husband. What's wrong with him? Why can't ...?" Mrs Mory couldn't finish what she wanted to say.

Sandy shook her head. "I can feel your husband somewhere close. But ... something is ... Something's wrong."

"What is it? What's wrong?" Mrs Mory wanted to know.

"Is it Billy?" Emma Fay asked. "Is he all right?"

Sandy started shaking. She pulled a face like she was in pain. The horrible noises started getting louder again. "Nat," she shouted at me, "get the glass, quickly!"

Mrs Tucker and Mr Coil didn't know what to do. Mrs Mory and Emma Fay kept asking questions, getting more and more worried. I jumped up to find the glass in Sandy's bag and put it upside down on the table in the middle of everyone.

"Keep the circle of hands," I said. "Don't move!" The noises were the loudest they'd ever been.

The four people were pale and scared. No one knew what was happening. Emma Fay was trying to back away but Mr Coil wouldn't let go of her hand.

"You've got to keep the circle!" I warned her.

"Please, Emma," Sandy said. "There's an evil spirit in the room with us. What we have to do is trap it in the glass. But the glass needs to be inside the circle of hands."

At last Emma Fay did as she was asked.

"You know what to do, Nat," Sandy said. "Hurry."

I nodded and leaned across the table to put my hand on the glass. As soon as I did the glass started moving under my palm. It was trembling and shuddering as it slipped across the table. I had to use both of my hands just to keep it still.

"Everyone close your eyes," Sandy said. "And think of the people you love. Think hard about how much you love them."

It seemed impossible but the noises got louder.

"Picture them in your minds," Sandy shouted. "Send them all your love. With every thought you have, think of them!"

Sandy reached out to put her hand on top of mine.

And suddenly the glass shattered. Broke into a thousand pieces. Exploded across the room.

Mrs Mory screamed. Mr Coil swore. Mrs Tucker and Emma Fay jumped up.

But the noises stopped and the light bulb Sandy was holding went out. The only sound we could hear in the room was our own heavy breathing.

Chapter 3
The Fox and the Photos

I opened the curtains and at last let some bright November light into the room. I wanted to get out as soon as we could.

At last the four people at the table let go of each other's hands. There was shattered glass on the table and the floor.

"I'm sorry I couldn't contact your husband," Sandy said to Mrs Mory. "The evil spirit was blocking him."

Mrs Mory was hot and fussed. "What happened? I don't understand. Why couldn't I talk to my husband? Is he all right?"

"I think so, yes," Sandy said. "I'm too tired to try again now, but we'll come back another day just to make sure."

Mrs Mory wasn't happy. "Well, I hoped today was the day. I so much wanted to talk to him again."

"What about Billy?" Emma Fay wanted to know.

"Billy's fine," Sandy said. "He helped us trap the evil spirit in the glass. He's very strong."

Emma Fay smiled, but only for a moment. Even so, it was the first time she'd smiled all day.

Mrs Tucker was setting her hat back on top of her head, but her fingers were trembling. Mr Coil was brushing splinters of glass from the front of his jumper. He mopped at his sweaty face with his handkerchief. "Was that meant to happen?" he asked.

"When the glass smashes," Sandy told him, "the spirit has to go back to where it came from. But we do need to come here again to be sure your husband is safe, Mrs Mory."

"I'll think about it," Mrs Mory said. "I just don't know what my husband would be doing with an evil spirit. It's not at all like him."

Mrs Tucker shook her head. "He wasn't that sort of man."

"It could be something in the house itself," Sandy said.

"There's nothing wrong with my house!" Mrs Mory was clearly upset.

Sandy nodded. She smiled. "I understand it's hard for you just now. Keep our phone number, in case you ever need it."

"Yes, yes, of course." Mrs Mory wasn't really listening. She was already taking us out of the room and back down the hall-way. She stopped suddenly at the door and put a hand to her mouth.

"Oh, my," she gasped. "Oh, my, oh, my."

We all crowded behind her to see. The stuffed fox was standing on the floor. It blocked our way and stared at us with its glassy eyes. It had moved all by itself somehow. Or something had moved it.

Mrs Tucker grabbed hold of Mrs Mory's arm. "Come away, dear," she said. "Come away from it."

Emma Fay shivered and hugged her arms around herself.

I stepped forward and prodded the fox with my shoe. It was still dead. "It's OK," I told them and I bent down to pick it up. "It must have been the spirit trying to scare us."

"Well, it bloody well worked," Mr Coil said. He tried to comfort Emma Fay by stroking her hair. She edged away from him. I didn't like his buttery moon-face and knew I wouldn't want him to stroke my hair. There was something strange about him.

I stood on a chair to put the fox back up on the top shelf. But that was when Mrs Mory saw the photos. All of the pictures of her husband had been turned around to face the wall. The old lady went pale when she saw them. She looked as if she might faint. Sandy rushed forward to help her.

"Don't worry," Sandy said. "I can tell just from his photos that your husband's a man with powerful energy. He'll be safe until Nat and I come back."

"Yes. Yes, you must come back," Mrs Mory said. "As soon as you can."

I walked along the hall and turned all the photos back the right way round. By the front door I put the light bulb back in the small lamp.

"Thank you. Thank you, so much," Mrs Mory said. She was all smiles now. She held onto Sandy's hand. "You're such a special young lady. You're so wise for your age."

Everyone agreed. Mrs Tucker, Mr Coil and Emma Fay. Then they paid her. £100 from each of them.

We shook hands. Mr Coil kept hold of Sandy's hand for too long as he told her how special she was. At last we waved good-bye and walked away down Turn Lane. When we were far enough away for no one to hear us, Sandy turned to me and grinned.

"You're brilliant, Nat," she said with a wink. "That fox was brilliant."

Chapter 4
What Really Happened

Everyone said my mother had a gift. They said she could talk to the dead.

But she couldn't. And nor can Sandy.

It's all a trick. A scam. A lie.

The light bulb is easy. You can buy trick bulbs that glow by themselves from most joke shops. They have batteries and a tiny switch. When I went out of the room to go and get the bulb from the lamp by the front door, all I did was take the real bulb and give Sandy the trick one. I kept the real bulb in my pocket, and just put it back in the lamp when we left.

The noises are more difficult. But that's why Sandy wears a long skirt all the way down to the floor. Under the skirt there are bits of metal tied to her ankles and inside her knees. She rubs them together to make the horrible metal noises. Then, on top of her knees, are two thick bits of wood. She knocks under the table with them.

Sandy walks in that floaty way so that nothing makes a sound by accident. It took her a long time to learn how to walk like that. It took even longer for her to learn how to keep the top of her body totally still while she moves her legs about under the table and makes all the noises. She can do it perfectly now.

How did Sandy know that Emma Fay's friend Billy had died? She didn't. But everyone who wants to talk to the dead talks about someone who's died. Sandy let Emma Fay do most of the talking. It was Emma Fay who told Sandy about Billy. And it was Emma Fay who talked about her gold ring.

The glass is a fake as well. It's not made out of real glass. It's made out of sugar-glass. It looks like normal glass, but it smashes more easily and won't cut you. They use the same stuff in movies. When an actor falls through a window, or smashes a bottle over someone's head, that window and that bottle are made out of sugar-glass.

When I put my hand on the glass and it moves around the table, it's me who's moving the glass. Then when Sandy puts her hand on top too, we can easily smash it. It's so simple, but it looks scary when it happens. And no one ever checks if it's real glass. Why would they? Who's going to lick smashed glass to see if it tastes like sugar?

What about the fox and the photos? How did they move?

Why do you think it took me so long to unscrew one light bulb? We always do something with photos if we can, but the fox was great. It was too good an idea to miss. And what I did with it worked really well.

So that's all Ghosting is. A lie. All you have to do is make people see or hear what they want to. If the room's dark, if the mood's right, it's not difficult. It's the easiest thing in the world to make people believe in something they want to believe in.

We have lots of different tricks. Mum taught them all to us. She used to go Ghosting a lot. And Sandy always helped her. Then, when Mum died, I started to help Sandy.

Sandy and I had been Ghosting by ourselves for over a year, and we'd made a lot of money. But I wasn't so happy any more.

When we got home from Turn Lane I tried to tell Sandy how I felt.

"£400," she said. "How can you be unhappy with £400?" She sat on the sofa in the living room, to untie all the metal and wooden noise-makers from her legs.

I gave a shrug. "I think we really scared them today. We might have gone too far."

"We have to scare them," Sandy said. "That way we get to go back and earn ourselves more money. Mrs Mory wants us back for two things now. One, to talk to her husband. And two, because she's really upset about evil spirits. Honestly, Nat, that fox was a brilliant idea."

I felt bad, not brilliant.

"We're not telling them they have to believe us, are we?" Sandy said. She dropped the metal and the wood on the floor and rubbed at her legs. "They already believe in ghosts and spirits anyway, don't they? Stupid people believe in stupid things. Not our fault, is it?" She picked up the TV remote and switched the TV on.

Part of me really wished Sandy could speak to the dead. Then maybe we could talk to Mum again.

"Mum never did things this way. She always said she was helping, putting people's minds at ease."

"Yeah, well, Mum's not here any more, is she?" Sandy snapped.

She sulked for a while, then said, "You wait, Nat. I bet we get all four of them wanting a Ghosting now. I bet Emma Fay is the first, wanting to talk to Billy again."

But Sandy was wrong. One week later it was Mr Coil who rang us up.

Chapter 5
A Private Ghosting

It was raining the day we went to Mr Coil's house. It was a small house, out of town, nothing nearby except fields. When he opened his front door he squinted at us from behind his little, round glasses.

"You're on time," he said. "Excellent. Come on in, why don't you?"

I'd told Sandy that I didn't think we should come here, but she hadn't listened. I'd said that I didn't like Mr Coil, that there was something strange about him. I didn't like the way he kept touching Emma Fay. He gave me the creeps. Sandy said he'd promised to pay £200, and there was no way she was going to say no to £200.

"Let me take your wet things," Mr Coil said and he helped Sandy take off her jacket.

His house was a lot smaller than Mrs Mory's. Her house had been dusty and full of stuff, but Mr Coil's was spotless. The walls were painted, but there was nothing on them. No bookshelves, no books, no photos. At the end of the hall-way there was a set of stairs which went up to the next floor. There were three doors in the hall-way. Two of them were open. One was the kitchen, which I could just see. It was as spotless and clean as everything else. The second door was for a room with a sofa and an armchair. It must have been a living room but I couldn't see a TV or anything. The third door was closed.

When we walked along the hall towards the kitchen, Sandy stopped and put her hand on the closed door.

"Is everything all right, my dear?" Mr Coil asked.

Sandy frowned. "I ... I think so," she said.

Mr Coil squeezed himself in between Sandy and the door. She had to take a step back.

"Sandy?" I asked. I didn't know what she was doing. Was she trying to pass me a secret message, like when she put her finger-tips over Mrs Mory's photos?

But she gave a shrug and smiled. "I'm fine, Mr Coil," she said. "Sorry. Please, lead the way."

I tried to catch her eye – what was she up to? She wouldn't look back at me.

"You'll have to forgive me," Mr Coil said, as he took us into his kitchen. "I'm not as lucky as Mrs Mory. My house is not as grand at all. No dining room for me. We'll have to settle for the kitchen table, if that's all right."

"Of course," Sandy said.

The table looked brand new to me. In fact the kitchen was all so clean it felt like a hospital. There were no packets or jars on the shelves, no washing-up liquid or tea-towel by the sink. There was no microwave or kettle.

How could anyone live with no mess or clutter? It was so clean it was weird. I looked down at my shoes and saw I'd left a track of muddy footprints on the white floor. Because of the rain outside, the room was dim anyway, but Mr Coil pulled the blinds shut and made it darker still.

"Are we waiting for the others?" Sandy asked.

"No, no," Mr Coil said. "I hope you don't mind if it's just me today."

Sandy and I looked at each other. There were nearly always three or four people.

"I really wanted to know more about your gift and I needed to see it close up," Mr Coil said. He smiled with his mouth, but not with his piggy eyes. "A private Ghosting, as it were. I'm very interested to hear what the dead have to say to me. On my own." He pulled a light bulb out of his pocket. "And I already have one of these ready and waiting for you."

Again Sandy and I looked at each other. All sorts of alarm bells were ringing in my head. I thought this man was going to catch us. He was going to try and prove how fake we really were.

Sandy took the bulb and thanked him. "It will be difficult with just you, Mr Coil," she said. She was very polite but I knew she was thinking and worrying the same as me. "You can't make a circle of hands by yourself."

Mr Coil sat at the table. "Then your brother can join me," he said.

Sandy nodded. I tried to tell her with my eyes that I wanted to be anywhere else but here. But she didn't take any notice. Mr Coil was already sitting, his hands held up ready to take mine. I sat down opposite him. I asked myself if he had a camera set up to film our tricks. Maybe Sandy would make it look as if she was trying her best, then simply pretend the dead didn't want to make contact today. Maybe she could say the house felt all wrong. Because it did feel wrong, even to me.

I took Mr Coil's hands and gripped them across the table. His hands were damp, greasy, limp.

"Who would you like me to contact for you?" Sandy asked.

Mr Coil gave a thin smile. "Whoever you can."

I could see Sandy was trying not to let Mr Coil see how awkward she felt. She held the light bulb he'd given her and tilted her head back. "Think of those people special to you, Mr Coil," she said. "Think of who you'd like to talk to once again."

I watched Mr Coil. He stared at my sister. I wanted Sandy to hurry up and finish. We could make excuses and go.

We were all silent, waiting. I could hear the rain against the outside of the window. Sandy closed her eyes. She began to rock in her chair – just a little. Mr Coil blinked twice, quickly. A tiny drop of sweat ran down his forehead, in between his eyes. He was nervous too, but trying to hide it. I could feel his grip on my hands tighten.

Of course the light bulb didn't glow. And there were no spirit noises. But suddenly Sandy screamed.

I was so shocked I jumped in my seat and let go of Mr Coil's hands. Sandy was gritting her teeth. Her eyes sprang wide open and she screamed again. And again.

Mr Coil seemed surprised too, but he reached across the table towards me. "Shouldn't we be holding hands?" he said.

I did as he asked, yet I couldn't take my eyes off Sandy. I'd never seen her act like this before. Even I had shivers running up and down my spine.

She was gasping for breath. She dropped the light bulb to the table. It bounced and rolled to the edge, then fell off onto the floor. It exploded with a bang when it hit the white tiles. And then Sandy fell forward onto the table, her hair over her face.

Mr Coil was gripping me hard but I pulled away from him and helped Sandy to her feet. I kept asking over and over if she was all right, but she wouldn't answer. Or couldn't answer. She was crying. Strands of her long hair stuck to her wet cheeks.

"We have to go," I told Mr Coil. I helped Sandy to get out of the kitchen and along into the hall.

Mr Coil wasn't happy. "What about your money?" he asked. "I want to pay you, at least."

I shook my head. I didn't want it. Something was wrong with Sandy. What I wanted was to get her as far away from him as I could. But as we passed the closed door in the hall she pushed me away and stood up tall. Once again she put her hand to the door. It was as if she was feeling for something behind it.

"I don't think you should go," Mr Coil was saying. "Your sister's not well. Stay – maybe I can help. Maybe she needs to rest."

I ignored him. I yanked Sandy away from the door and dragged her out of the house into the rain.

Chapter 6
The Other Side of the Door

I wished Mum was here. Mum would have known what to do. Life was difficult without her and I missed her so much. She would have told Sandy to calm down and think about what she was doing.

Sandy did seem better when we got back home, but now she was talking rubbish.

"It was real," she said. She was sitting on the edge of the sofa, her head in her hands. "I felt ... I don't know what I felt. Maybe it was a ghost. But there was something bad, too. Something really horrible."

I couldn't sit down. I walked to and fro across the living room. "We lie," I told her. "That's what Mum did, that's what we do. We trick people. We don't even believe in ghosts."

Sandy looked up at me. "I'm not lying, Nat. You've got to believe me. Something got inside my head."

"So why now?" I asked her. "Why, after all these years, after all of the times you've been Ghosting with Mum and me, why suddenly now do you think you felt a ghost?"

"Maybe this time was the first time there really was a ghost." She gave a shrug. "Maybe his house really was haunted."

I didn't know what to say. I couldn't answer her.

"We have to go back," Sandy said. "It was behind that door. The one he kept closed. Something was behind that door and I have to know what it was."

"No way," I said. "Listen to yourself. You can't go back."

"I'll go without you if I have to," Sandy said.

So that night, we went all the way back out of town to Mr Coil's house.

It was nearly midnight, cold and still raining. We waited under a tree by the side of the road and watched the house. There was no car in the driveway, no lights on in the windows, no movement at all.

"He's not home," Sandy said.

"We should try the bell anyway," I said.

"I'll try," Sandy said. Before I could stop her she was running up the drive. She pressed the bell and ducked around the side of the house, where no one could see her. Nothing happened. No one came to the door. Sandy waved at me to come up to the house.

"Maybe he doesn't live here," I said when I reached her. And that made sense to me. "No one could live in a house and keep it as clean and tidy as that. He didn't have any stuff to be able to live with anyway. No TV, no microwave. Not even any washing-up liquid."

Sandy nodded. "We still need to be careful," she said.

We headed round to the back door and the kitchen. We crouched in the shadows and Sandy picked up a rock.

"Are you sure you want to do this?" I asked.

Sandy nodded. "Keep watch round the front," she told me.

I pulled my collar up to keep off some of the rain, but also to hide as much of my face as I could. I thought about Mum. She was a fake, a fraud. But she wasn't a house-breaker. What were we doing here? I leaned around the corner of the house and watched the road. But this far out of town there were no cars. And the fields on either side were empty.

It all made the noise of smashing glass even louder. I was scared. My head told me to run. But I waited until I heard Sandy whisper my name. She had broken a small window in the back door. She reached in and unlocked the door. Most of the time when we smashed glass it was to "send evil spirits away". This felt like we were walking into where the evil spirits came from.

At least the noise we'd made was the last bit of proof that Mr Coil wasn't in the house. He'd have come running if he was. We waited to listen, but no one came. Everything was still, silent.

Sandy went quickly over to the closed door in the hall-way. I stayed in the kitchen for a moment or two. I saw someone had cleaned up my muddy shoe prints from the floor, and swept up the broken glass from the light bulb too. I opened one of the drawers to see if there were knives and forks, but the first drawer was empty. So were the second and the third. There were no cups or plates in the cupboards. When I pulled the fridge door open the light inside didn't even come on. The fridge wasn't plugged in.

"He can't live here," I said to Sandy as I came into the hall. "There's nothing here."

She was rattling the handle of the closed door, but it was locked. "We need to break it open," she said.

I still wasn't sure. "Can you feel anything now?" I asked. "Like you did this afternoon?"

She nodded. "It's filling up my skull. It's pushing at the sides of my head. And whatever it is feels like it's coming from behind this door."

"What if there's nothing there?"

"Then I'm wrong. Or mad or something. But first I have to see."

I was worried. If we broke the door down then Mr Coil would know we'd been here. Did it matter? After all, we'd just smashed the window in the back door and my finger-prints were all over the kitchen. There was no going back now.

Sandy and I kicked at the door hard. After four or five good solid whacks it burst open. There was a set of stairs leading down to a pitch-black basement. On the top step was a torch and Sandy picked it up, switched it on.

The beam of light lit up the stairs all the way to the bottom. The basement was 100 per cent different from the rest of the house. Up here the house was spooky because of how spotless and clean it was. Down there it was horrific because of the amount of blood that was splashed across the walls and floor.

Chapter 7
Ring-finger

We both stood totally still. For a long time we just couldn't move. We didn't want to go down those stairs into that basement, but we both knew we had to.

Sandy was white. She was trembling. She held a hand up to her head. "My head feels like it's going to burst," she said. "I think someone died down here, and their spirit's trying to get into my head. I'm not pretending any more. This is for real."

We didn't want to touch the walls, and we had to be careful where we stepped so we went together down the stairs very slowly. The basement was small and stuffy. Sandy moved the torch around us in little sweeps. The torch beam lit up a work-bench with three different saws on top and all of them were spattered with red. Next the torch beam showed a stack of six square plastic crates. The crates were big, but not big enough to fit a whole body. And then we saw something on the floor – a hand. It still had fingers. One of the fingers still wore a ring. It glinted in the torch-light.

Sandy let out a sob. "Emma," she said. "Emma Fay!"

I knew she was right and my belly filled with ice. "We have to get the police," I said.

We both turned to go back up the stairs, but Sandy let out a screech of pain and dropped the torch. The torch went out as it hit the floor and I had to scrabble about with my hands to find it. I was scared of the blackness of the basement and scared that the torch was broken. I snatched it up as soon as I found it. I had to shake it and hit it on my hand to get the light to flicker on again. At last the strong beam shot out in front of me. I pointed the light at our feet. That way we wouldn't see the sick things around us.

Sandy looked ill with pain.

"Are you OK?" I asked. "What's wrong?"

"My head. Something inside my head won't let me leave this place."

It was hard to keep my fear under control. "We have to go. We need to call the police." I put my hand in my pocket to get my mobile. I tried to hold the torch and press the numbers on my mobile at the same time, but my fingers were clumsy. I swore at myself, tried to force myself to stay calm.

Sandy had both hands to her head. "She won't let me go. It's Emma. She's inside my head and she needs me to stay here."

Was this really happening? Was my sister going mad? All I knew was that we had to get out.

999. I put my phone to my ear. "Hello? Hello? Police?" I grabbed at Sandy and pulled her back up the stairs.

She fought me and my phone flew out of my hand. It flew away into the darkness. "Sandy!" I screeched.

"She's there!" Sandy shouted and pointed to the far corner of the pitch-black basement.

I spun around with the torch, but the corner was empty.

"I can see her," Sandy said. "She's huddled up. Her arms are around her knees and she's crying. I can see her. She's so scared. Look, she's trying to get away." Sandy turned suddenly and pointed at the opposite corner of the basement.

I was quick to turn too. I spun the torch's beam across the darkness. "I can't see her."

"She's running. She's trying to escape from him." Sandy was turning this way and that.

I tried to follow with the torch but I couldn't see anything. "I can't see her. I can't see her!"

"That's because she's already dead," Sandy said, and burst into tears.

The fear was rising from my belly and filling my throat. I tried to swallow it away. I needed to find my phone. "Come on. Please, Sandy. Help me."

And that was when we heard the front door slam. Footsteps came along the hall-way. Before we even had time to hide, Mr Coil was standing at the top of the stairs.

He slowly took off his glasses and polished them with his handkerchief. Then he used the same handkerchief to mop his sweaty brow.

"You came back," he said. "I'm so pleased."

Chapter 8
Scared to Death

Mr Coil's moon-face glowed in the beam of the torch. His glasses glinted. He stepped down the stairs towards us.

"Stay back," I warned him. "Stay back."

He gave a low chuckle and licked his lips. "Why? What will you do to me?"

"I'll call the police," I said. Even I could tell how pathetic I sounded.

Mr Coil stopped at the bottom of the stairs. He picked something up. "Call the police?" he asked. "With this, I suppose?" He'd found my mobile. He tut-tutted and slipped the mobile into his pocket. "I think not," he said.

"Stay back. I've got a knife," I lied.

Mr Coil didn't believe me. He started to come towards us. "Even if you do have a knife, do you think you'll be brave enough to use it? I don't think so, young man."

"What do you want?" I asked. "What are you going to do?"

"I'm going to enjoy killing you," he said. "Both of you."

My hand shook. I couldn't keep the torch still. I hated myself. Anyone could see I was scared to death.

"If you want my sister, you'll have to get past me first," I spat out. The torch's beam was steady at last. "And I don't think you can do that, old man."

Sandy was on her knees next to me. She was holding her head and her whole body was shaking. Something was happening to her. Something strange.

Mr Coil stared at us. He knew I'd put up a fight. "Maybe I'll let your sister go," he said. "Maybe I won't."

"Don't come any closer," I told him.

"It's my hobby," he said. "Young people. But I do believe in ghosts, and I do believe my young people keep coming back to haunt me. They cry so loudly at night I can't sleep. They whisper horrible things to me. I had to move house to get away from them."

I glared at him. What was he saying? Did he want me to feel sorry for him?

"It was a bit of luck when I met the pair of you at Mrs Mory's house," Mr Coil went on. "I was only there because my new young friend, Emma, took me. But when I saw you and your sister get rid of that evil spirit, I thought I could ask you to help me. I was so sad this afternoon when I found out you were both fakes."

"Stay back!" I shouted.

But he wasn't scared of me. He looked as if he was going to make a grab for me.

Then Sandy shouted, "I can't bear it! There are so many of them!"

I turned to look at her. And could hardly believe what I saw.

She was on fire. A blue, flickering fire was wrapped around her body. Inside the fire I could see faces. They were the faces of teenagers. They swirled around her, their mouths open in silent screams. I didn't need the torch now. The dead ghost-light filled the basement. It was a cold blue, an icy blue of death. But as I watched, the fire turned red. The colour of blood and pain.

I tried to grab Sandy but I couldn't move her. Mr Coil began to step backwards up the stairs. He waved his hands in front of him, trying to keep the ghosts away. He slipped, stumbled back then tried to stand up again.

I could make out one of the faces in the ghost-light. It was the face of Emma Fay. Emma's face went over Sandy's so that I couldn't see Sandy any more. The other spirits boiled around her.

Mr Coil was stood helpless on the stairs. Then the swirling spirits dived from my sister towards him. He shouted out and held his hands above his head to protect himself. But the angry ghosts smothered him. He was lost underneath them. He screamed, but his shouts didn't come out. The spirits had clogged up his throat. He tried to kick and punch, but the churning spirits held him down.

They swarmed over him like rats. They bit and ripped at him.

He squirmed beneath them and tried to fight. He lost his glasses. They fell and shattered. He struggled but it was no good. He was getting weaker. His face was a mask of terror. He couldn't fight the ghosts any more. He tried to escape one last time. And he tumbled to the floor. His head fell back and his arms and legs twisted under him. He gave a shudder. His eyes were wide – wide and white. Then at last he was still.

The ghost-light vanished.

Once more the basement was dark. I shone the torch on Mr Coil. He was dead. He lay on his back with blank eyes that stared at the blood on the walls.

Sandy was panting. I helped her stand up. "Can you walk?" I asked her.

She nodded. "I'm OK, I think ..."

"You sure?" I had to help her stand.

"My head's empty now. They've all gone. I just feel ..." She shook her head. "I want to get out of here."

We left Mr Coil exactly as he'd fallen. Sandy was worn out and weak. I had to half-carry her up the stairs, then out of the house and into the cool night air. The cold rain made my face tingle. I felt very alive. And was glad to be out of that house. But Sandy still didn't look well.

"What happened in there?" I asked.

"I think it was Emma Fay," Sandy said.

"I saw her face," I said.

Sandy nodded. "She believed me when we were at Mrs Mory's. She believed I really could talk to the dead. When we came here this afternoon, she tried to force her way into my head. It was her I could feel trying to call me. But it was only when we came back tonight that she could fully get inside me."

"Inside your head?" I asked.

"Yes. And once she was in there, I couldn't stop the others from getting inside me too. It was like she broke down a wall in my head, and then there was this sudden flood of other ghosts. They needed me so they could cross over into our world and ... And do what they did."

"Mr Coil's dead," I said.

Sandy nodded. "Yes. They did it."

"Do you think he murdered them all?" I whispered.

Sandy stared at her feet and started to cry. "Call the police, Nat. There are families out there missing their loved ones. They need to know what's happened."

That was when I remembered. My phone was in Mr Coil's pocket.

Chapter 9
Broken

I didn't want to leave Sandy, but I knew I had to get my phone from Mr Coil. If the police found it then we'd be part of everything that had happened in that basement. There were our finger-prints too. Should I try and wipe clean everything we'd touched? We didn't want the police to come and ask us any questions. What if they found out about how Sandy faked talking to the dead?

Sandy wasn't well. She looked white and sick, and kept holding her head as if it hurt her. I told her I was going to get my phone. But she couldn't hear me.

"Sandy," I said, louder. I shook her arm. "Sandy? Did you hear what I said?"

She looked at me as if I was a long way away. Then slowly her eyes came into focus again. "My head hurts, Nat. It feels like something inside has broken open. It's like I've got a big, empty cave in my mind."

"You'll be OK," I said. Was that true? I didn't know. "Everything's going to be fine," I went on.

Sandy was drifting away from me again. "Echoes," she said. "It's like a cave full of echoes, right here in my head."

She was making me scared. "Wait for me," I said. "Just wait here. I'll be as quick as I can." I ran back into the house. I wanted to get my phone, get Sandy home, and have everything back to normal.

I took my T-shirt off and wiped everything I could remember touching in the kitchen. The drawers and the fridge, the light switch, the door handle. I did everything twice. Then I took a deep breath, switched the torch on and went back down into that terrible basement.

The torch beam lit up Mr Coil's body. I knew he was dead, but it felt like he was watching me with his blank, open eyes. I walked down the stairs, one step at a time. I wanted to be quick. I'd just grab my phone and go, but my fear slowed me down.

I thought I heard a noise. I flashed the torch's beam around the basement but there was no one else there. Just blood on the walls, Emma Fay's white hand on the floor, and those plastic crates. I had to hold my breath to stop myself from being sick.

I knew Mr Coil was dead but I had to prod him with my foot to make sure. He didn't twitch or moan. So I crouched down next to him. His blank eyes stared beyond me now, as if they were looking at someone else standing behind me. I had to look behind me too. Was there anyone? I aimed the torch back up the stairs. But no one was there. Of course no one was there.

I told myself to stop being stupid, to hurry up. I put my hand inside one of Mr Coil's pockets ... And nearly cried out.

His pocket was full of hair. Dark hair like Emma Fay's. Tied with a small red bow. I dropped the hair on the floor.

I had to roll Mr Coil over to get at his other pocket. I put my T-shirt over my hands and pushed him. He was heavy. His eyes now stared up at the dark ceiling.

I pulled his coat out from under him to get at the other pocket. I gritted my teeth. This time I shone the torch into the pocket first. There was my phone. And nothing else.

Then I heard someone shouting. Upstairs, outside the house. It was Sandy. Sandy was screaming.

I grabbed my phone and ran back up the stairs. I charged out of the house but couldn't see Sandy at first. The rain was heavy now and the night had got even darker. When she screamed again I saw she was out in the middle of the road. I ran towards her, shouting her name.

She was in a panic, terrified. "Can't you see them?" she shouted. "Can't you see them?"

"See what?" I asked. "Sandy? What can you see?"

"Look!" she said. "They're all around us!"

But we were alone on a country road in the middle of the night.

"Sandy ..." I didn't know what to say. "I don't understand."

"Ghosts," she said. "All around us."

"From Mr Coil's?" I asked.

Sandy shook her head. "From everywhere. They're coming to me from everywhere. They want me to help them but I can't. There're so many of them. Emma Fay broke into my head and now I can't keep them out."

She was turning around, stepping out of the way, trying to move past things I couldn't see. It was like she was in the middle of a crowd of people that no one else could see.

"I can't help you," she shouted at thin air. "I can't do anything!"

I grabbed her. I needed to calm her down. "We pretend," I told her. "We're liars, remember? Mum couldn't talk to ghosts, and neither can you. We're just fakes."

Sandy was weeping. She stared me in the eye. "No, Nat," she said. "Not any more."